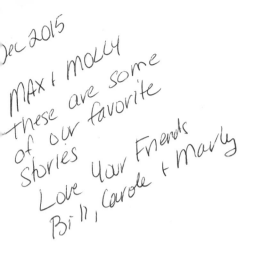

Dec 2015

MAX + MOLLY
these are some
of our favorite
Stories

Love Your Friends

Bill, Carole + Marly

MUNSCH
Mini-Treasury One

by Robert Munsch and Michael Kusugak
art by Michael Martchenko
and Vladyana Langer Krykorka

annick press
toronto • new york • vancouver

Cover illustration by Michael Martchenko
Cover designed by Sheryl Shapiro
Sixth printing, October 2015

We acknowledge the support of the Canada Council for the Arts, the Ontario Arts Council, and the Government of Canada through the Canada Book Fund (CBF) for our publishing activities.

ONTARIO ARTS COUNCIL
CONSEIL DES ARTS DE L'ONTARIO
an Ontario government agency
un organisme du gouvernement de l'Ontario

Cataloging in Publication

Munsch, Robert N., 1945-
    Munsch mini-treasury. One / by Robert N. Munsch and Michael Kusugak ; art by Michael Martchenko and Vladyana Langer Krykorka.

Contents: The paper bag princess — Angela's airplane — 50 below zero — A promise is a promise — Pigs.
ISBN 978-1-55451-273-7

    1. Children's stories, Canadian (English). I. Kusugak, Michael II. Martchenko, Michael III. Krykorka, Vladyana IV. Title.

PS8576.U575M8497 2010   jC813'.54   C2010-902014-6

Printed and bound in China.

For e-book editions of classic Robert Munsch stories, please visit annickpress.com/ebooks

visit us at: **www.annickpress.com**
visit Robert Munsch at: **www.robertmunsch.com**

CONTENTS

The Paper Bag Princess

Story
Robert N. Munsch

Illustrations
Michael Martchenko

Where did This Story come from?

The Paper Bag Princess was first told at the Bay Area Childcare Center in Coos Bay, Oregon, where Robert Munsch worked. He had been telling lots and lots of dragon stories where the prince saves the princess from the dragon. One day, his wife asked him, "How come you always have the prince save the princess? Why can't the princess save the prince?" He thought about it and changed the ending of one of his dragon stories. As for the name Elizabeth, when a little girl with that name came to the daycare for the first time, she dropped her coat on the floor and waited for her teacher to hang it up. Munsch thought, "Wow! This kid thinks she's a princess." And that's how the princess in the book came to be called Elizabeth.

★ ★ ★

To Elizabeth

Elizabeth was a beautiful princess. She lived in a castle and had expensive princess clothes. She was going to marry a prince named Ronald.

Unfortunately, a dragon smashed her castle, burned all her clothes with his fiery breath, and carried off Prince Ronald.

Elizabeth decided to chase the dragon and get Ronald back.

She looked everywhere for something to wear, but the only thing she could find that was not burnt was a paper bag. So she put on the paper bag and followed the dragon.

He was easy to follow, because he left a trail of burnt forests and horses' bones.

Finally, Elizabeth came to a cave with a large door that had a huge knocker on it. She took hold of the knocker and banged on the door.

The dragon stuck his nose out of the door and said, "Well, a princess! I love to eat princesses, but I have already eaten a whole castle today. I am a very busy dragon. Come back tomorrow."

He slammed the door so fast that Elizabeth almost got her nose caught.

Elizabeth grabbed the knocker and banged on the door again.

The dragon stuck his nose out of the door and said, "Go away. I love to eat princesses, but I have already eaten a whole castle today. I am a very busy dragon. Come back tomorrow."

"Wait," shouted Elizabeth. "Is it true that you are the smartest and fiercest dragon in the whole world?"

"Yes," said the dragon.

"Is it true," said Elizabeth, "that you can burn up ten forests with your fiery breath?"

"Oh, yes," said the dragon, and he took a huge, deep breath and breathed out so much fire that he burnt up fifty forests.

"Fantastic," said Elizabeth, and the dragon took another huge breath and breathed out so much fire that he burnt up one hundred forests.

"Magnificent," said Elizabeth, and the dragon took another huge breath, but this time nothing came out. The dragon didn't even have enough fire left to cook a meatball.

Elizabeth said, "Dragon, is it true that you can fly around the world in just ten seconds?"

"Why, yes," said the dragon, and jumped up and flew all the way around the world in just ten seconds.

He was very tired when he got back, but Elizabeth shouted, "Fantastic, do it again!"

So the dragon jumped up and flew around the whole world in just twenty seconds.

When he got back he was too tired to talk, and he lay down and went straight to sleep.

Elizabeth whispered, very softly, "Hey, dragon." The dragon didn't move at all.

She lifted up the dragon's ear and put her head right inside. She shouted as loud as she could, "Hey, dragon!"

The dragon was so tired he didn't even move.

Elizabeth walked right over the dragon and opened the door to the cave.

There was Prince Ronald. He looked at her and said, "Elizabeth, you are a mess! You smell like ashes, your hair is all tangled and you are wearing a dirty old paper bag. Come back when you are dressed like a real princess."

"Ronald," said Elizabeth, "your clothes are really pretty and your hair is very neat. You look like a real prince, but you are a bum."

They didn't get married after all.

Angela's Airplane

Story • Robert Munsch
Art • Michael Martchenko

Where did This STory come from?

Angela's Airplane was one of the original stories Robert Munsch told in the daycare in Coos Bay, Oregon. The idea came to him because one day at the daycare center, they were listening to the radio when the announcer said that a little girl named Candy was having a ride in an airplane as part of an air show. Candy was a friend of Munsch's, so he immediately made up a story about her. He changed the girl's name to Angela for the book, but now he wishes he had kept the name Candy.

★ ★ ★

To Candy Christianson

Angela's father took her to the airport, but when they got there, a terrible thing happened: Angela's father got lost.

Angela looked under airplanes and on top of airplanes and beside airplanes, but she couldn't find him anyplace, so Angela decided to look *inside* an airplane.

She saw one with an open door and climbed up the steps: one, two, three, four, five, six— right to the top. Her father was not there, and neither was anyone else.

Angela had never been in an airplane before. In the front there was a seat that had lots of buttons all around it. Angela loved to push buttons, so she walked up to the front, sat down in the seat and said to herself, "It's okay if I push just *one* button. Don't you think it's okay if I push just *one* button? Oh yes, it's okay. Yes, yes, yes, yes."

Then she slowly pressed the bright red button. Right away the door closed.

Angela said, "It's okay if I push just one more button. Don't you think it's okay if I push just one more button? Oh yes, it's okay. Yes, yes, yes, yes." Slowly she pushed the yellow button. Right away the lights came on.

Angela said, "It's okay if I push just *one more* button. Don't you think it's okay if I push just *one more* button? Oh yes, it's okay. Yes, yes, yes, yes." She pushed the green button. Right away the motor came on: VROOM, VROOM, VROOM, VROOM.

Angela said, "Yikes," and pushed all the buttons at once. The airplane took off and went right up into the air.

When Angela looked out the window, she saw that she was very high in the sky. She didn't know how to get down. The only thing to do was to push one more button, so she slowly pushed the black button. It was the radio button. A voice came on the radio and said, "Bring back that airplane, you thief, you."

Angela said, "My name is Angela. I am five years old and I don't know how to fly airplanes."

"Oh dear," said the voice. "What a mess. Listen carefully, Angela. Take the steering wheel and turn it to the left."

Angela turned the wheel and very slowly the airplane went in a big circle and came back right over the airport.

"Okay," said the voice, "now pull back on the wheel."

Angela pulled back on the wheel and the airplane slowly went down to the runway. It hit once and bounced. It hit again and bounced. Then one wing scraped the ground. Right away the whole plane smashed and broke into little pieces.

Angela was left sitting on the ground and she didn't even have a scratch.

All sorts of cars and trucks came speeding out of the terminal.

There were police cars, ambulances, fire trucks and buses. And all sorts of people came running, but in front of everybody was Angela's father.

He picked her up and said, "Angela, are you all right?"

"Yes," said Angela.

"Oh, Angela," he said, "the airplane is not all right. It is in very small pieces."

"I know," said Angela, "it was a mistake."

"Well, Angela," said her father, "promise me you will never fly another airplane."

"I promise," said Angela.

"Are you sure?" said the father.

Angela said, very loudly, "I promise, I promise, I promise."

Angela didn't fly an airplane for a very long time. But when she grew up, she didn't become a doctor, she didn't become a truck driver, she didn't become a secretary and she didn't become a nurse. She became an airplane pilot.

50 Below Zero

Story by Robert Munsch
Art by Michael Martchenko

Where did This Story come from?

50 Below Zero was first told in a town called Watson Lake in Yukon Territory. Robert Munsch went there during Children's Book Week to visit schools; however, when he got there, no one knew he was coming. The airport was about ten miles outside of Watson Lake, but it was 50 below zero and he wasn't going to walk to town. He finally got the school principal to pick him up at the airport and take him to a hotel. The next day, at the school in Watson Lake, there were signs on the walls telling the children to be careful of frostbite. Munsch said to himself, "These kids would like a story about cold." So he made up *50 Below Zero*, and the kids loved it.

★ ★ ★

To Jason, Watson Lake,
and Tyya, Whitehorse, Yukon Territory

In the middle of the night, Jason was asleep: zzzzz—zzzzz—zzzzz—zzzzz—zzzzz.

He woke up! He heard a sound. He said, "What's that? What's that? What's that!"

Jason opened the door to the kitchen ...

and there was his father, who walked in his sleep. He was sleeping on top of the refrigerator.

Jason yelled, "PAPA, WAKE UP!" His father jumped up, ran around the kitchen three times, and went back to bed.

Jason said, "This house is going crraaazy!" And he went back to bed.

Jason went to sleep: zzzzz—zzzzz—zzzzz—zzzzz—zzzzz.

He woke up! He heard a sound. He said, "What's that? What's that? What's that!"

He opened the door to the kitchen. No one was there.

He opened the door to the bathroom ...

and there was his father, sleeping in the bathtub.

Jason yelled, "PAPA, WAKE UP!" His father jumped up, ran around the bathroom three times, and went back to bed.

Jason said, "This house is going crraaazy!" But he was too tired to do anything about it, so he went back to bed.

Jason went to sleep: zzzzz—zzzzz—zzzzz—zzzzz—zzzzz.

He woke up! He heard a sound. He said, "What's that? What's that? What's that!"

He opened the door to the kitchen. No one was there. He opened the door to the bathroom. No one was there. He opened the door to the garage ...

and there was his father, sleeping on top of the car.

Jason yelled, "PAPA, WAKE UP!" His father jumped up, ran around the car three times, and went back to bed.

Jason said, "This house is going crraaazy!" But he was too tired to do anything about it, so he went back to bed.

Jason went to sleep: zzzzz—zzzzz—zzzzz—zzzzz—zzzzz.

He woke up! He heard a sound. He said, "What's that? What's that? What's that!"

He opened the door to the kitchen. No one was there. He opened the door to the bathroom. No one was there. He opened the door to the garage. No one was there. He opened the door to the living room. No one was there.

But the front door was open, and his father's footprints went out into the snow— and it was 50 below zero that night.

"Yikes," said Jason, "my father is outside in just his pajamas. He will freeze like an ice cube."

So Jason put on three warm snowsuits, three warm parkas, six warm mittens, six warm socks, and one pair of very warm boot sort of things called mukluks. Then he went out the front door and followed his father's footprints.

Jason walked and walked and walked and walked. Finally he found his father. His father was leaning against a tree.

Jason yelled, "PAPA, WAKE UP!"

His father did not move.

Jason yelled in the loudest possible voice, **"PAPA, WAKE UP!"**

His father still did not move.

Jason tried to pick up his father, but he was too heavy.

Jason ran home and got his sled. He pushed his father onto the sled and pulled him home. When they got to the back porch, Jason grabbed his father's big toe and pulled him up the stairs: *bump, bump, bump, bump.*

He pulled him across the kitchen floor: *scritch, scritch, scritch, scritch.* Then Jason put his father in the tub and turned on the warm water.

glug.

glug,

glug,

glug,

glug,

The tub filled up: glug,

Jason's father jumped up and ran around the bathroom three times and went back to bed.

Jason said, "This house is going crazy. I am going to do something." So he got a long rope and tied one end to his father's bed and one end to his father's big toe.

Jason went to sleep: zzzzz—zzzzz—zzzzz—zzzzz—zzzzz.

He woke up! He heard a sound. He said, "What's that? What's that? What's that!"

He opened the kitchen door ...

and there was his father, stuck in the middle of the floor.

"Good," said Jason, "that is the end of the sleepwalking. Now I can get to sleep."

In the middle of the night, Jason's mother was asleep: zzzzz—zzzzz—zzzzz—zzzzz—zzzzz.

She woke up! She heard a sound. She said, "What's that? What's that? What's that!"

She opened the door to the kitchen and ...

A PROMISE IS A PROMISE

Story • Robert Munsch & Michael Kusugak
Art • Vladyana Krykorka

Where did This Story come from?

Whenever Robert Munsch went to the Northwest Territories, he would stay in Rankin's Inlet with the family of children's book author Michael Kusugak. Michael started telling him Inuit stories that are used to warn children of dangers. One story, about a monster who lives under the ice, reminds children to be very careful to avoid cracks in the ice. Other monsters who live on the tundra grab kids as soon as their parents can't see them. This story is told to keep kids from getting lost and freezing to death. Later, Michael sent him a story about his own meeting with one of the ice monsters. Munsch said, "Hey, this is pretty neat." He and Michael worked on it together for a long time until they finally had a story they were both happy with, called *A Promise is a Promise*.

★ ★ ★

To Julia Muckpah, Eskimo Point, N.W.T.,
who started the whole thing
Robert Munsch

To my sons Qilak, Ka'lak and Arnanajuk
Michael Kusugak

On the very first nice day of spring Allashua said, "I'm going to go fishing. I'm going to go fishing in the ocean. I'm going to go fishing in the cracks in the ice."

"Ah, ah," said her mother, "don't go fishing on the sea ice. Under the sea ice live Qallupilluit. They grab children who aren't with their parents. Don't go fishing in the ocean. Go fish in a lake."

"Right," said Allashua. "I promise to go fishing in the lake and not in the ocean, and a promise is a promise."

So Allashua set out like she was going to go to the lake near her house, but when she got to the end of the street, she didn't go to the lake. She walked down the long snowy path that led to the ocean.

At the edge of the ocean were large cracks where the tide broke and jumbled the ice. Allashua looked very carefully and did not see any Qallupilluit. She said, "On TV I have seen Santa Claus, Fairy Godmothers and the Tooth Fairy, but never any Qallupilluit. I think my mother is wrong."

But just in case her mother was right, Allashua stood beside the sea ice and yelled, "Qallupilluit have dirty noses."

Nothing happened.

Allashua yelled, "Qallupilluit smell like a dead whale in the summer."

Nothing happened.

Allashua walked right out onto the sea ice and yelled, as loud as she could, "Qallupilluit, Qallupilluit can't catch me!"

Nothing happened. The only thing Allashua heard was the sound of snow blowing over the ice.

So Allashua got out her line and her hook. She walked over to a large crack in the ice and started to fish. Right away a fish grabbed the hook and Allashua pulled it up. She caught six fish in a row.

Allashua yelled, "I am the best fisherman in the world!"

And from behind her something said, with a voice that sounded like snow blowing over the ice, *"The best you may be, but the smartest you are not."*

Allashua turned around. There, between her and the shore, were the Qallupilluit. They looked at her and said, *"Have you seen the child who said Qallupilluit have dirty noses?"*

"Oh, no, Qallupilluit. I have seen no such child, and besides, your noses are very pretty."

"Have you seen the child who said we smell like a dead whale in the summertime?"

"Oh, no, Qallupilluit. I have seen no such child, and besides, you smell very nice, just like flowers in the summer."

"Have you seen the child who yelled, 'Qallupilluit, Qallupilluit can't catch me'?"

"Oh, no, Qallupilluit. I have seen no such child, and besides, my mother says that you can catch whatever you want to."

"Right," said the Qallupilluit. *"We catch whatever we want to, and what we want to catch right now is you."*

One grabbed Allashua by her feet and dragged her down, down, under the sea ice to where the Qallupilluit live.

The sea water stung Allashua's face like fire. Allashua held her breath and the Qallupilluit gathered around her and sang, with voices that sounded like snow blowing over the ice:

Human child, human child
Ours to have, ours to hold.
Forget your mother, forget your father;
Ours to hold under the ice.

Allashua let out her breath and yelled, "My brothers and sisters, my brothers and sisters; I'll bring them all to the sea ice."

For a moment nothing happened, and then the Qallupilluit threw Allashua up out of the sea into the cold wind of the ice and said, *"A promise is a promise. Bring your brothers and sisters to the sea ice and we will let you go."*

Allashua began to run up the long, snow-covered path that led to her home. As she ran, her clothes started to freeze. She ran more and more slowly, until she fell to the ground. And that is where Allashua's father found her, almost at the back door, frozen to the snow.

Allashua's father gave a great yell, picked up Allashua and carried her inside. He tore off Allashua's icy clothes and put her to bed. Then the father and mother got under the covers and hugged Allashua till she got warm. After an hour Allashua asked for some hot tea. She drank ten cups of hot tea with lots of sugar and said, "I went to the cracks in the sea ice."

"Ah, ah," said her family, "not so smart."

"I called the Qallupilluit nasty names."

"Ah, ah," said her family, "dumber still."

"I promised to take my brothers and sisters to the cracks in the sea ice. I promised to take them all to the Qallupilluit."

"Ah, ah," said her family, "a promise is a promise." Then her mother and father made some tea and they sat and drank it, and didn't say anything for a long time.

From far down the snow-covered path that led to the sea, the Qallupilluit began calling, *"A promise is a promise. A promise is a promise. A promise is a promise."*

The mother looked at her children and said, "I have an idea. Do exactly as I say. When I start dancing, all of you follow Allashua to the cracks in the sea ice."

And the children all whispered to each other, "Ah, ah, why will our mother dance? This is not a happy time."

Allashua's mother went out the back door and yelled, "Qallupilluit, Qallupilluit, come and talk with me."

And they did come, right up out of the cracks in the sea ice. Up the long, snow-covered path to the sea they came, and stood by the back door. It was a most strange thing, for never before had the Qallupilluit left the ocean.

The mother and father cried and yelled and asked for their children back, but the Qallupilluit said, "A promise is a promise."

The mother and father begged and pleaded and asked for their children back, but the Qallupilluit said, "A promise is a promise."

Finally Allashua's mother said, "Qallupilluit, you have hearts of ice; but a promise is a promise. Come and join us while we say goodbye to our children."

Everyone went inside. First the mother gave her children some bread. She said to the Qallupilluit, "This is not for you." But the Qallupilluit said, *"We want some too."* The mother gave the Qallupilluit some bread, and they liked it a lot.

Then the mother gave each of her children a piece of candy. She said to the Qallupilluit, "This is not for you." But the Qallupilluit said, *"We want some too."* The mother gave the Qallupilluit some candy, and they liked it a lot.

Then the father started to dance. He said to the Qallupilluit, "This is not for you." The Qallupilluit said, "We have never danced. We want to dance." And they all started to dance. First they danced slowly and then they danced fast, and then they started to jump and yell and scream and dance a wild dance. The Qallupilluit liked the dancing so much that they forgot about children.

Finally the mother started to dance, and when the children saw their mother dancing, they crawled out the back door and ran down the long, snowy path that led to the sea. They came to the cracks in the sea ice and Allashua whispered, "Qallupilluit, Qallupilluit, here we are."

Nothing happened.

Then all the children said, "Qallupilluit, Qallupilluit, here we are."

Nothing happened.

Then all the children yelled, as loud as they could, "Qallupilluit, Qallupilluit, here we are!"

Nothing happened, and they all went back to the land and sat on a large rock by the beach.

Two minutes later the Qallupilluit ran screaming down the path and jumped into their cracks in the ice. Allashua stood up on the rock and said, "A promise is what you were given and a promise is what you got. I brought my brothers and sisters to the sea ice, but you were not here. A promise is a promise."

The Qallupilluit yelled and screamed and pounded the ice till it broke. They begged and pleaded and asked to have the children, but Allashua said, "A promise is a promise." Then the Qallupilluit jumped down to the bottom of the sea and took their cracks with them, and the whole ocean of ice became perfectly smooth.

Then the mother and father came walking down the long, snowy path to the ocean. They hugged and kissed each one of their children, even Allashua. The father looked at the flat ocean and said, "We will go fishing here, for Qallupilluit have promised never to catch children with their parents, and a promise is a promise."

Then they all did go fishing, quite happily. Except for Allashua. She had been too close to the Qallupilluit and could still hear them singing, with voices that sounded like blowing snow:

> *Human child, human child*
> *Ours to have, ours to hold.*
> *Forget your mother, forget your brother;*
> *Ours to hold under the ice.*

The End

A Qallupilluq is an imaginary Inuit creature, somewhat like a troll, that lives in Hudson Bay. It wears a woman's parka made of loon feathers and reportedly grabs children when they come too near cracks in the ice.

The Inuit traditionally spend a lot of time on the sea ice, so the Qallupilluit were clearly invented as a means to help keep small children away from dangerous crevices.

Michael Kusugak, thinking back to his childhood in the Arctic, made up a story about his own encounter with the Qallupilluit. He sent it to Robert Munsch, who had stayed with Michael's family while telling stories in Rankin Inlet, N.W.T. *A Promise is a Promise* is the result of their collaboration.

PIGS

Story by Robert Munsch
Art by Michael Martchenko

Where did This sTory come from?

Robert Munsch was telling stories in a school way out in the country when he got the idea of making up a story about farm animals. He asked the class if anyone lived on a farm. Lots of kids put up their hands. He chose one girl named Megan who said they had sheep on their farm. "Maybe I can make up a story about that," thought Munsch. So he wrote a story about sheep, but after two years of telling it, he started changing around the kinds of animals in the story. He used chickens and cows, horses and donkeys, and finally he used pigs. It turned out that pigs worked better than anything else—kids found them the funniest of all.

★ ★ ★

To Meghan Celhoffer
Holland Centre, Ontario

Megan's father asked her to feed the pigs on her way to school. He said, "Megan, please feed the pigs, but don't open the gate. Pigs are smarter than you think. Don't open the gate."

"Right," said Megan. "I will not open the gate. Not me. No sir. No, no, no, no, no."

So Megan went to the pig pen. She looked at the pigs. The pigs looked at Megan.

Megan said, "These are the dumbest-looking animals I have ever seen. They stand there like lumps on a bump. They wouldn't do anything if I did open the gate." So Megan opened the gate just a little bit. The pigs stood there and looked at Megan. They didn't do anything.

Megan said, "These are the dumbest-looking animals I have ever seen. They stand there like lumps on a bump. They wouldn't even go out the door if the house was on fire." So Megan opened the gate a little bit more. The pigs stood there and looked at Megan. They didn't do anything.

Then Megan yelled, "HEY YOU DUMB PIGS!"
The pigs jumped up and ran right over Megan,
WAP—WAP—WAP—WAP—WAP,
and out the gate.

When Megan got up she couldn't see the pigs anywhere. She said, "Uh-oh, I am in bad trouble. Maybe pigs are not so dumb after all." Then she went to tell her father the bad news. When she got to the house Megan heard a noise coming from the kitchen. It went, "OINK, OINK, OINK."

"That doesn't sound like my mother. That doesn't sound like my father. That sounds like pigs."

She looked in the window. There was her father, sitting at the breakfast table. A pig was drinking his coffee. A pig was eating his newspaper. And a pig was peeing on his shoe. "Megan," yelled her father, "you opened the gate. Get these pigs out of here."

Megan opened the front door a little bit. The pigs stood and looked at Megan. Finally Megan opened the front door all the way and yelled, "HEY YOU DUMB PIGS!" The pigs jumped up and ran right over Megan, WAP—WAP—WAP—WAP—WAP, and out the door.

Megan ran outside, chased all the pigs into the pig pen and shut the gate. Then she looked at the pigs and said, "You are still dumb, like lumps on a bump." Then she ran off to school. Just as she was about to open the front door, she heard a sound: "OINK, OINK, OINK."

She said, "That doesn't sound like my teacher. That doesn't sound like the principal. That sounds like pigs."

Megan looked in the principal's window. There was a pig drinking the principal's coffee. A pig was eating the principal's newspaper. And a pig was peeing on the principal's shoe. The principal yelled, "Megan, get these pigs out of here!"

Megan opened the front door of the school a little bit. The pigs didn't do anything. She opened the door a little bit more. The pigs still didn't do anything. She opened the door all the way and yelled, "HEY YOU DUMB PIGS!" The pigs jumped up and ran right over Megan, WAP—WAP—WAP—WAP—WAP, and out the door.

Megan went into the school. She sat down at her desk and said, "That's that! I finally got rid of all the pigs." Then she heard a noise: "OINK, OINK, OINK." Megan opened her desk, and there was a new baby pig. The teacher said, "Megan! Get that dumb pig out of here!"

Megan said, "Dumb? Who ever said pigs were dumb? Pigs are smart. I am going to keep it for a pet."

At the end of the day the school bus finally came. Megan walked up to the door, then heard something say, "OINK, OINK, OINK."

Megan said, "That doesn't sound like the bus driver. That sounds like a pig." She climbed up the stairs and looked in the bus. There was a pig driving the bus, pigs eating the seats and pigs lying in the aisle.

A pig shut the door and drove the bus down
the road.

It drove the bus all the way to Megan's farm,
through the barnyard and
right into the pig pen.

Megan got out of the bus, walked across the barnyard and marched into the kitchen. She said, "The pigs are all back in the pig pen. They came back by themselves. Pigs are smarter than you think."

And Megan never let out any more animals.

At least, not any more pigs.

Books in the Munsch for Kids series:

The Dark
Mud Puddle
The Paper Bag Princess
The Boy in the Drawer
Jonathan Cleaned Up, Then He Heard a Sound
Murmel, Murmel, Murmel
Millicent and the Wind
Mortimer
The Fire Station
Angela's Airplane
David's Father
Thomas' Snowsuit
50 Below Zero
I Have to Go!
Moira's Birthday
A Promise is a Promise
Pigs
Something Good
Show and Tell
Purple, Green and Yellow
Wait and See
Where is Gah-Ning?
From Far Away
Stephanie's Ponytail
Munschworks
Munschworks 2
Munschworks 3
Munschworks 4
The Munschworks Grand Treasury
Munsch Mini-Treasury One
Munsch Mini-Treasury Two

For information on these titles please visit www.annickpress.com
Many Munsch titles are available in French and/or Spanish. Please
contact your favorite supplier.